CARLETON PLACE
PUBLIC LIBRARY

THE NUMBERLYS

BY WILLIAM JOYCE & CHRISTINA ELLIS

MOONBOT
books

A
atheneum

ATHENEUM BOOKS FOR YOUNG READERS   New York   London   Toronto   Sydney   New Delhi

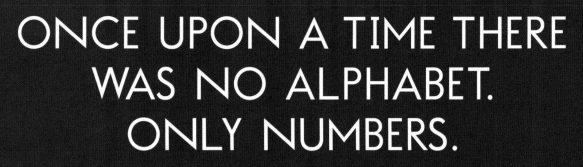

ONCE UPON A TIME THERE WAS NO ALPHABET. ONLY NUMBERS.

EVERYONE LIKED NUMBERS.
THEY HAD NICE SHAPES AND
KEPT THINGS ORDERLY.
AND EVERYTHING ADDED UP....
SO LIFE WAS SORT OF....
NUMBERLY.

STREETS WERE CALLED BY THEIR NUMBERS, AS WERE TOWNS, COUNTRIES—EVERYTHING.

BUT THERE WEREN'T ANY
BOOKS OR COLORS
OR JELLYBEANS OR PIZZA.
ONLY 00267, WHICH WAS
THICK AND GRAY AND GLOOPY,
AND 00268, WHICH WAS THICKER
AND GRAYER AND, WELL....
GLOOPIER.

BUT THERE WERE 5 FRIENDS WHO HAD BEEN THINKING, FOR MORE DAYS THAN THEY COULD COUNT, WONDERING IF THEY COULD DO SOMETHING....

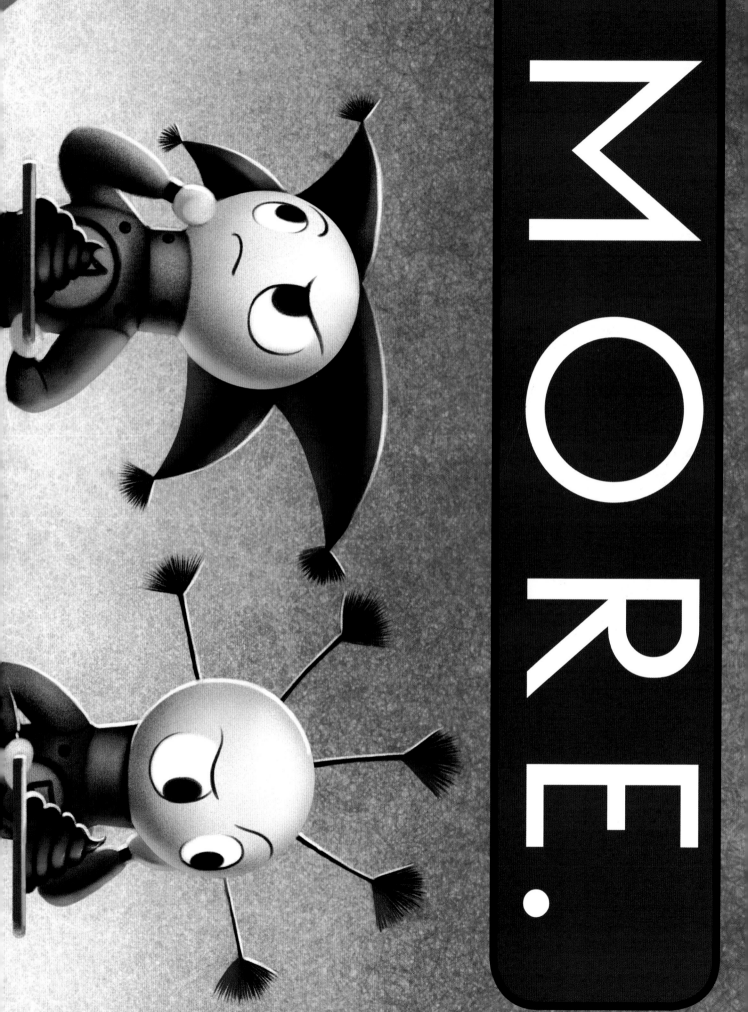

MAYBE THEY NEEDED SOMETHING...

DIFFERENT.

SO THEY
STARTED TO
WORK.

AT FIRST IT WAS AWFUL.

THEN . . . :
ARTFUL.

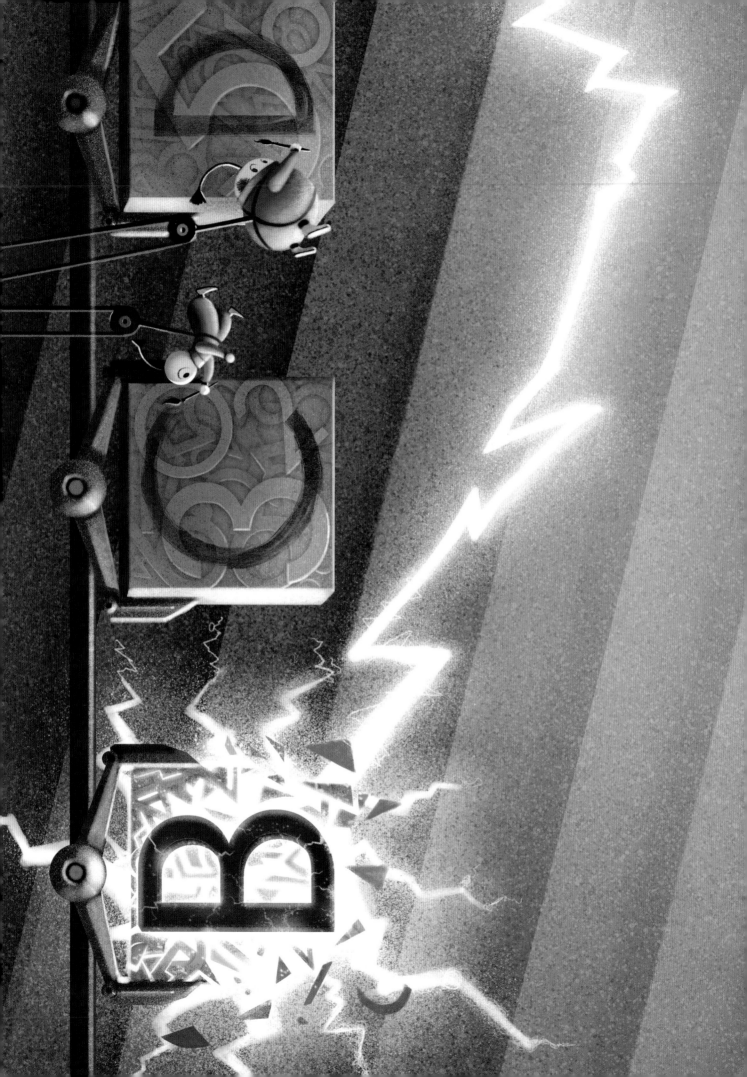

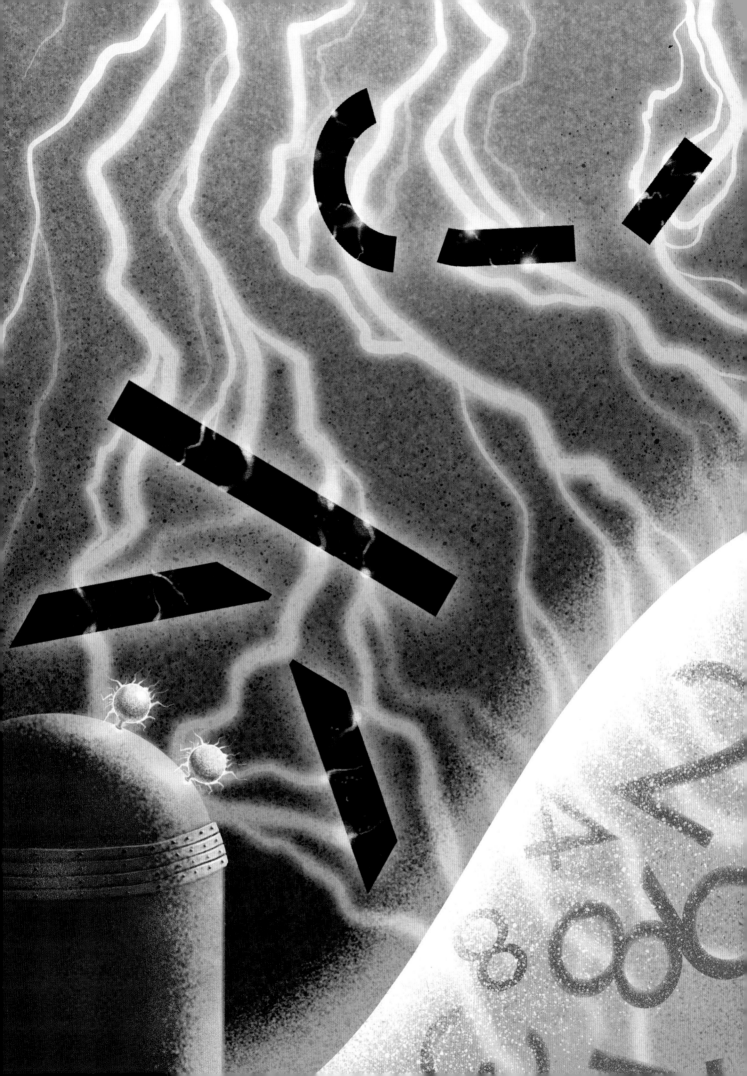

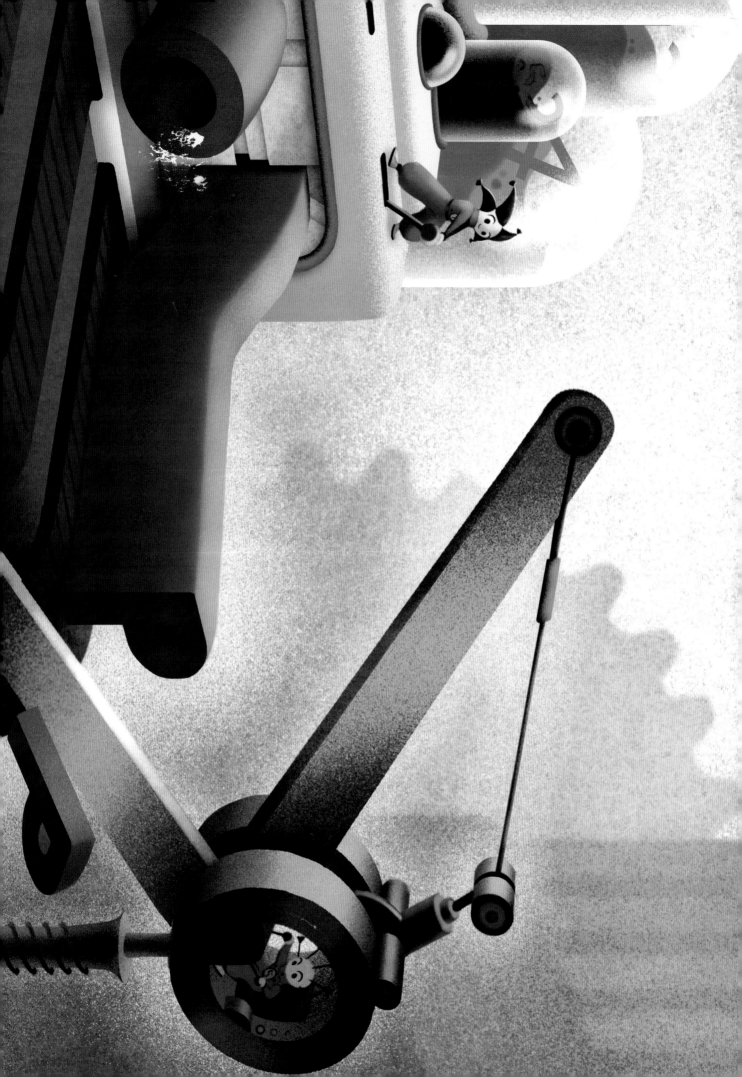

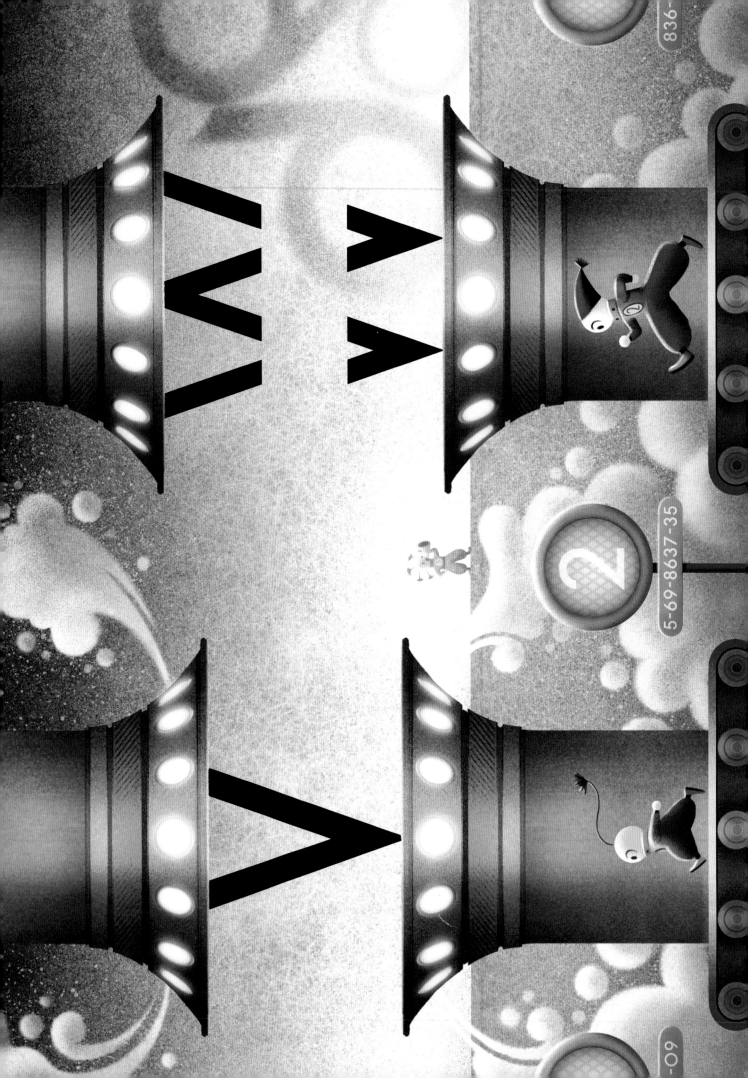

WHEN THEY CAME TO THE LAZT LETTER, THINGZ BEGAN TO HAPPEN...

AND THEY KNEW IT WAS TIME TO SHOW THE NUMBERLY WORLD.

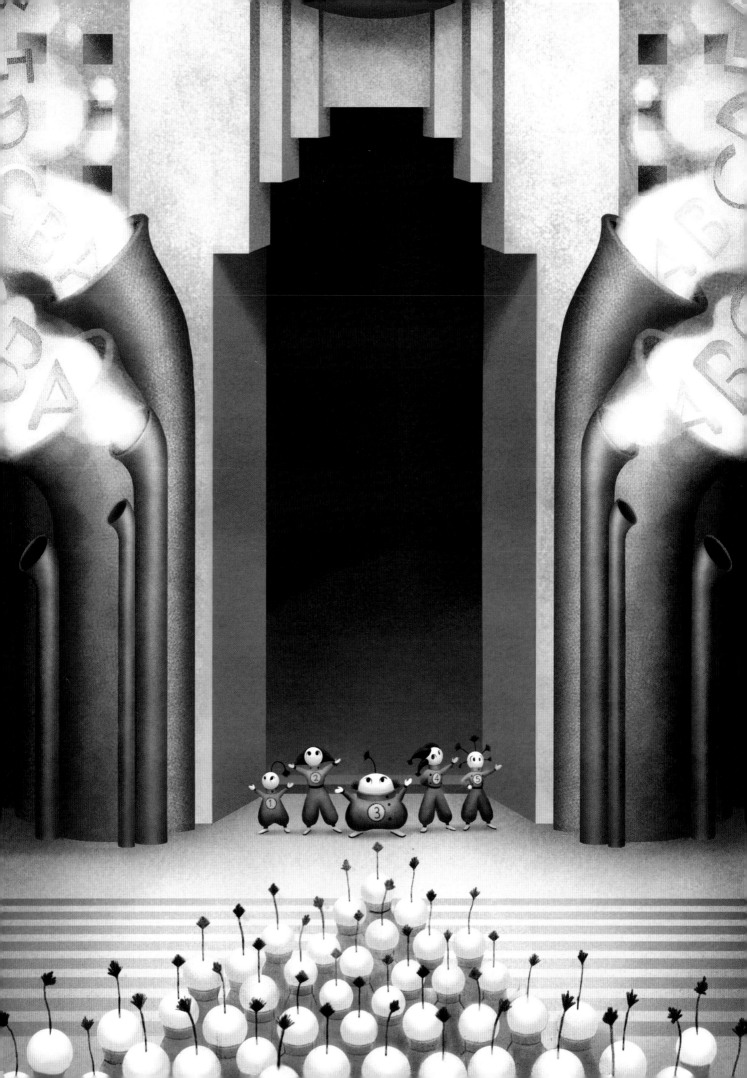

SUDDENLY THE LETTERS FORMED INTO WORDS, AND AS THEY FORMED WORDS, THE WORLD WAS FILLED WITH AMAZEMENTS!

AS THE DAY ENDED, THE FIVE WERE SLEEPY BUT SATISFIED. THEY HAD DONE SOMETHING NEW, SOMETHING DIFFERENT, SOMETHING MORE!